The Sapphire Princess Helps a Mermaid

THE JEWEL KINGDOM

The Sapphire Princess Helps a Mermaid

JAHNNA N. MALCOLM

Illustrations by Paul Casale

SCHOLASTIC INC.
NEW YORK   TORONTO   LONDON   AUCKLAND   SYDNEY
MEXICO CITY   NEW DELHI   HONG KONG

ISBN 0-590-97878-0

12 11 10 9 8 7 6 5 4 3 2 1   9/9 0 1 2 3 4/0

Printed in the U.S.A.   40
First Scholastic printing, January 1999

For
Mom, Dad, Charlie,
and Aunt Gertie.
Thanks for believing!

CONTENTS

———◆◆◆———

The Sapphire Princess Helps a Mermaid

THE JEWEL KINGDOM

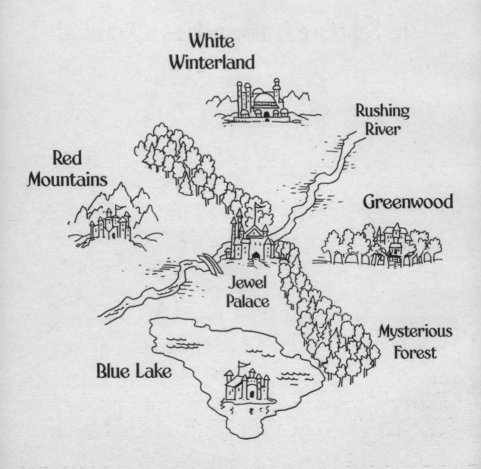

White
Winterland

Rushing
River

Red
Mountains

Greenwood

Jewel
Palace

Mysterious
Forest

Blue Lake

A Surprise Catch

Princess Sabrina stood at the window of the Sapphire Palace, watching the waters of Blue Lake. She was expecting a very important visitor, a Mermaid named Atlanta. Atlanta lived beneath the ocean with her parents and three sisters. She and Sabrina had been friends since they were little.

The Sapphire Princess and her friends

had spent an entire week getting ready for Atlanta's visit. They had planned a costume ball for the first evening and everyone had worked together to decorate the palace. The Storkz brought reed flowers that grew only in the Misty Marsh. The Nymphs and Water Sprites strung beautiful paper lanterns everywhere. Breads were baked and cakes were decorated. Finally everything was finished.

But Atlanta wasn't there yet. She was very late. And Sabrina was starting to get nervous.

Sabrina shook her long blonde hair over her shoulders and took a deep breath.

I'm just excited, she told herself. That's what is making my skin tingle.

Sabrina watched the weeping willow trees dip their branches in Blue Lake. The sun shone brightly. Blue Nymphs played by the palace bridge. But still she couldn't stop worrying about Atlanta.

The princess thought she heard a noise behind her. She turned to look. No one was there.

But there was a small puddle of water on the floor. The puddle was striped with rainbows.

"That's odd," Sabrina murmured as she bent to wipe it up. "Rainbows in puddles mean something, but I can't remember what."

"Who are you talking to?" a voice called from the door.

Sabrina looked up to see a purple-and-yellow butterfly fluttering above her head. It was Zazz, her palace advisor and best friend.

"Zazz!" she cried. "I'm glad you're here. Has our guest arrived?"

Zazz shook her head. "Not yet."

The Sapphire Princess crossed to the window. "They were supposed to be here an hour ago." Sabrina had sent Titus, her palace guard, to escort Atlanta to Blue Lake. And Gurt the Gilliwag and Shallow the Nymph were with him.

Zazz fluttered onto Sabrina's shoulder. "It's a long way from the Undersea to the Jewel Kingdom. Be patient."

"It's hard to be patient," Sabrina replied. "I'm just so excited about seeing Atlanta. The last time I saw her was when her family came to my coronation at the Jewel Palace."

"That was a very big day," Zazz said with a nod. "It was when you and your three sisters were crowned the Jewel Princesses."

On that day, Sabrina had become the

Sapphire Princess. Her sisters, Roxanne, Emily, and Demetra, had been crowned the Ruby, Emerald, and Diamond Princesses. Then each was given her own land to rule.

"Atlanta has never been to Blue Lake," Sabrina said. "I can't wait to show her around."

Zazz fluttered to the window in Sabrina's room. "Oh, look, Princess. I see boats and banners. Atlanta must finally be here!"

Crash!

A loud noise came from the hall outside Sabrina's bedroom.

"What was that?" Zazz squeaked.

"I don't know," Sabrina whispered. "But let's find out."

The Sapphire Princess raced into the hall with Zazz flying behind her. Two more rainbow-colored puddles dotted the floor.

"Look, Zazz, more water." Sabrina frowned as she followed the puddle down the hall. "Why can't I remember what those rainbows mean?"

"They're a magical sign," Zazz squeaked.

The puddles led Sabrina to the Throne Room. It was built of white marble. In the center was a deep pool that flowed into Blue Lake.

Just as Sabrina came in, she heard a splash.

Sabrina grabbed hold of a wooden crank and lowered a net into the water. "Someone just dove into the pool," she called to Zazz. The net jerked in her hands. "But I think I've got him."

"Good catch, Princess," Zazz cried.

"Pull him up and let's take a look at the intruder."

As Sabrina pulled on the net, rainbow colors stretched across the water.

Suddenly she remembered what the rainbows meant. "Water and rainbows always appear whenever —"

"What have you caught?" Zazz cut in as the net burst out of the water.

Sabrina stared at the silvery blue fish tail swishing back and forth in her net.

"A Mermaid," she gasped.

Atlanta

———◦━◦◦━◦———

 The Mermaid wriggled back and forth in the net. Her long red hair flowed like seaweed across her milky skin. She clutched the net with her fingers and turned to look at the Sapphire Princess.

"Atlanta!" Sabrina cried. "It's you."

Without thinking, Sabrina dropped the net. The Mermaid fell back into the water with a loud splash.

Atlanta struggled free of the net and swam to the edge of the pool. "Why did you do that?" she sputtered.

"I am so sorry." Sabrina put her hands to her face. This visit was getting off to a bad start. "I'm just so surprised to see you."

Zazz fluttered over the Mermaid's head. "We've been waiting for you for over an hour."

"That's right," Sabrina added. "And I thought you were with Titus."

"Titus?" Atlanta repeated. "Well, I seem to have lost him."

Sabrina knelt on the edge of the pool. "Lost him? Did something happen on your trip?"

"Well . . ." Atlanta twisted a strand of red hair between her fingers. "That's a long story."

Sabrina smiled. Atlanta was famous for her stories. Ever since she was a little Mermaid she'd had a very big imagination. If Atlanta saw a whale, she said it was the largest whale in the ocean. If she found a pearl, she said it was the prettiest pearl in the world. Atlanta loved to exaggerate.

Atlanta's imagination was one of the reasons she was visiting Sabrina. Because she was one of four children, Atlanta's parents were convinced that she made up stories to make people notice her. They thought a visit to another kingdom would give her the attention she needed. They hoped Atlanta would finally stop making up her wild stories.

"Tell me the story," Sabrina said to her friend. "I'd love to hear it."

Atlanta looked over both shoulders and peered into the water below her before she spoke. "Titus and your friends came to get me in the Undersea. But just as we were leaving my kingdom, I saw a terrible creature following us."

"What kind of creature?" Sabrina asked.

Atlanta scrunched up her face trying to look like the creature. "He was a short little man with sharp teeth and big pointy ears. His eyebrows were green and his eyes shone yellow."

"Did you see the creature again?" Zazz asked.

Atlanta frowned. "Two more times. He swam beside us in the shadows."

"Did you tell Titus?" Sabrina asked.

Atlanta nodded. "I tried to show the others, but every time I'd cry 'There he is!' the creature would disappear. I was the only one who ever saw him. Titus didn't believe there was a creature at all."

Zazz perched on Sabrina's shoulder and whispered, "This sounds fishy, if you ask me."

"Zazz, hush!" Sabrina whispered back. "What happened next?"

The Mermaid swam in worried circles. "Sabrina, I was so afraid of that awful creature that I ran away from your friends. You have to hide me!" she cried. "I don't want that creature to find me!"

Sabrina knelt beside the pool. "Try to stay calm. Maybe this creature looks fierce but really means no harm."

"Princess!" a gruff voice called from the Throne Room door. "Princess, I need to speak to you!"

"It's Titus," Sabrina whispered.

The Mermaid's eyes filled with fear. "Please don't tell him I'm here," Atlanta begged. "He'll tell the others and that awful creature will find me."

"But, Atlanta — "

Atlanta dove into the water and vanished.

At the same instant, Titus came into the Throne Room. The Strider bowed at the waist and said, "Princess, I have terrible news. Atlanta the Mermaid has disappeared."

"No, she hasn't — " Zazz started to say, but Sabrina tapped the butterfly on the wing. Zazz stopped talking.

"Zazz is right," Sabrina said quickly. "Atlanta is fine. She, um, sent word that she needed to return home."

Titus raised one eyebrow. "Really? I wonder why she didn't tell us. We would

have escorted her back to the Undersea."

"I think she was in a hurry," Sabrina added.

The palace guard still looked confused. "It surprises me that she would go home on her own."

"Why?" Sabrina asked.

"Well, she seemed to be scared of so many things. First she thought she saw a Two-Headed Snag. Then she swore she'd seen a Monstrous Grinder."

"Had she?" Zazz asked.

"No," Titus replied. "The first were two sleeping eels, and the second was just a large knob of coral."

Zazz looked at the princess, who could only shrug.

"Well, thank you, Titus, for your help," Sabrina finally said.

Titus bowed. "You're welcome,

Princess, but what about the celebration you've planned?"

Sabrina waved one hand. "Oh, that will still happen. Tell everyone to get ready for the ball."

"Very well, Princess," Titus said as he backed out of the room.

The instant Titus left the room, Zazz squeaked, "Why didn't you tell Titus the truth about Atlanta?"

Sabrina pointed to the pool and whispered, "Because Atlanta is my guest, and she asked me not to."

"Hmmph!" Zazz folded two of her legs across her chest. "I don't know if I believe her story about that funny little creature. You know you can't always believe what she says."

"Zazz!" Sabrina gasped. "Don't say such a thing."

"It sounds like Atlanta lied to Titus

about seeing monsters, and now she has you telling lies, too."

Sabrina frowned. Zazz was right. She had lied to Titus. But she had to protect her friend. Even if she liked to exaggerate.

Just then, Atlanta burst out of the water. "Thank you, Sabrina, for keeping my secret. I am very grateful."

Sabrina stared hard at her friend. Atlanta seemed to be sincere, in spite of what Zazz thought.

"We'll have to find another place to hide you," Sabrina said. "Too many people pass through the Throne Room."

"Where can I hide?" Atlanta asked.

Sabrina snapped her fingers. "I know just the place."

The Beautiful Shell

 Princess Sabrina's bathtub was the perfect hiding place for a Mermaid. It was large enough for Atlanta to stretch out in and even swim a little.

"No one will ever find you here," Sabrina said as Atlanta made herself comfortable.

"Good," Atlanta murmured. "Maybe

that terrible creature will go back to where he came from."

Sabrina looked out the windows of her bath. It was hard to imagine a strange little creature hiding in the lily pads or under the willow trees.

"Do you really think that creature followed you here?" Sabrina asked.

"Probably." Atlanta sunk low in her bath, so only her eyes were peeking above the water. "He was very sneaky."

Sabrina smiled at her friend. "Well, don't worry. This bath is the last place he'll look for you."

Atlanta wiggled her eyebrows. "Wait till my parents hear I spent my visit hiding in your bathtub."

Sabrina perched on a chair by the bathtub. "I hope you won't have to hide here for the entire visit."

Atlanta rested her elbows on the edge of the tub. "It's the perfect chance for us to talk."

Sabrina giggled. "You mean, tell each other secrets?"

Atlanta nodded eagerly. "And speaking of secrets, I hid something in your bedroom." The Mermaid pointed to a cabinet. "It's in there. Open the door and look inside."

Sabrina opened the cabinet. Inside was the prettiest seashell she'd ever seen.

"Oh, Atlanta!" she whispered, carrying the pink-and-gold conch to the bathtub. "This shell is beautiful."

"It's not only beautiful, it's magic," Atlanta said. "Hold it to your ear and listen."

Sabrina lifted the shell to her ear. "I can hear the ocean!"

"That's my ocean," Atlanta said proudly. "Would you like to hear my kingdom?"

"Oh, yes." Sabrina listened harder. Soon she heard voices. "Someone is talking," she said. "Girls. I can hear girls talking."

Atlanta pressed her ear to the shell. "Those are my sisters," she cried with delight.

"Where did you get such a marvelous shell?" Sabrina asked.

Atlanta slipped back into the bathwater. "I found it," she said.

"Really?" Sabrina rubbed her hand across the smooth pink-and-gold shell. "Where?"

"At the bottom of the Undersea," Atlanta said. "When I was hunting for a Snapping Lurch. I had to be very careful. A

Snapping Lurch has a terrible temper. If you make them angry they'll bite you with their big spiky teeth."

"I didn't think Lurches lived in the Undersea," Sabrina said, lowering the shell. "In fact, I'm sure they don't."

"Oh." Atlanta blew bubbles in the water. "That's probably why I never found one."

Sabrina was pretty sure her friend wasn't telling the truth. And this was the first one of Atlanta's stories that Sabrina didn't like. She didn't know why Atlanta would lie. But how could Sabrina question her? Atlanta was her guest.

Sabrina decided to change the subject. "I have a surprise for you, too."

"Oh, good!" Atlanta clapped her hands together. "What is it?"

"I'm giving you a ball," Sabrina said. "Everyone in Blue Lake is invited."

Atlanta frowned. "But I can't go to a ball. Someone might recognize me."

"No, they won't," Sabrina said. "This is a costume ball."

"You mean, I can wear a disguise?" Atlanta asked excitedly.

"Yes." Sabrina leaped to her feet. "I have yours in my wardrobe. Let me get it."

Sabrina hurried to her closet. Just as she opened the door, she heard Atlanta scream.

The Sapphire Princess raced to the bathroom and found Atlanta hiding behind a stack of towels.

"What is it?" Sabrina asked.

The Mermaid pointed toward the bathroom window. "That awful creature. He's here. I saw his face in the window!"

The Masked Ball

 The Sapphire Princess called for Zazz, and they whispered together while Atlanta put on her costume in the next room.

"She said she saw that strange creature at the window," Sabrina said, keeping her voice low. "But I didn't see him at all."

"Do you think she's making him up?" Zazz asked.

"I don't know," Sabrina said as she put

on her mask for the costume party. It was trimmed in peacock feathers that matched her shimmering blue gown. "Atlanta really seemed scared. But sometimes she exaggerates. I don't know what to believe."

"You said she made up a story about hunting for a Snapping Lurch," Zazz pointed out. "Maybe this is just another one of her stories."

"Sabrina!" Atlanta called from the other room. "I'm ready."

"What are you going to do?" Zazz hissed.

Sabrina crossed to the door. "I have to believe her, Zazz. She's my friend."

Atlanta was dressed in a beautiful swan mask. Her long red hair was tucked beneath a snow-white hood, and her mermaid tail was hidden under a white velvet cape. She sat in her own swan boat, which was a little carved wagon.

"Oh, Atlanta," Sabrina cried with glee. "It's a perfect disguise. No one will ever guess it's you."

Atlanta smoothed out her cape. "This way I can watch for that strange little creature, but he won't know it's me."

Zazz and Sabrina exchanged looks but said nothing.

Sabrina picked up the wagon's handle. "I'll pull your swan boat to the party."

Sabrina led the three of them down the long hall and into the palace garden. What she saw next made her laugh with delight.

Every creature in Blue Lake had come to the ball. They were all dressed in brightly colored costumes and beautiful painted masks.

Paper lanterns painted with water

lilies hung from the trees and hedges. An orchestra played on a floating dance floor crowded with dancers.

"I don't recognize a soul," Sabrina whispered to Zazz.

"I do." Zazz pointed to a guest disguised as a large rabbit. Two green froglike feet stuck out from under the furry costume. "Those could only belong to Gurt the Gilliwag."

Sabrina laughed. "You're probably right."

Suddenly Atlanta sat up in her wagon and shouted, "There he is! I see him!"

Sabrina spun around. "Where?"

Atlanta pointed impatiently. "There! In the gold jacket."

Sabrina saw a flash of gold disappear into the crowd.

"What are you waiting for?" Atlanta

cried. "Sabrina, follow that creature!"

The orchestra played a lively jig. More dancers leaped onto the dance floor. Atlanta cried out again.

"There he is! By the punch bowl."

Sabrina's eyes widened. A little creature in a golden suit *was* standing at the punch bowl. "I'll go get him."

She marched over and slapped her hand on the creature's shoulder. "State your name and business," she ordered. "Or I'll call a guard."

The creature turned in alarm. "It's me, Princess," he stammered, pulling off his goldfish mask. "Jetsam the Water Sprite. I'm just here to have fun."

Sabrina felt her cheeks turn bright red. "That's good, Jetsam," she said quickly. "I want everyone to have a wonderful time."

Jetsam hurried away and Sabrina

turned to look at her friend. Atlanta was sitting calmly in the swan wagon.

Suddenly Sabrina felt foolish. She had hurt Jetsam's feelings. And it was all Atlanta's fault. She couldn't seem to tell the truth. There was no strange little creature. Atlanta must have made him up to get attention.

"All right," Sabrina muttered. "If that's what she wants, she can have it!"

The Sapphire Princess leaped onto the stage beside the orchestra and raised her hand for them to stop. Taking off her peacock mask, she cried, "Greetings, everyone!"

All of the Blue Lake creatures recognized their princess and cheered.

"Are you having fun?" Sabrina asked.

"Yes!" they cried.

"I have a surprise for you," Sabrina

said. "You may have heard that our guest of honor couldn't join us tonight. But that's not true. She's right here and I'd like you all to meet her."

The swan wagon sat at the edge of the stage, just beside Blue Lake. Sabrina heard Atlanta gasp, "What are you doing?"

Sabrina didn't answer. Instead, she reached down and pulled off Atlanta's mask. "Here she is, everyone — Atlanta from the Undersea! Let's show her how happy we are she's here."

The crowd cheered again.

Atlanta stared at Sabrina with hurt in her eyes. "How could you?" she whispered.

Before Sabrina could say a word, Atlanta threw off her cape and dove into the water. With a splash she was gone.

Listen to the Shell

————◆————

Sabrina stared at the rings of water spreading across Blue Lake. They marked the spot where Atlanta had disappeared.

"Now I've done it," Sabrina murmured. "I was mad at Atlanta and I wanted her to know. But I didn't want her to run away!"

"You had better go after her," Zazz

said. "She doesn't know our land. She could get lost."

Sabrina looked at her party guests. They stood silent, waiting for her to tell them what to do.

"Please go on with the party," she called. "I'll find Atlanta and bring her back."

"I'll check the pools around the palace," Zazz said, fluttering above the water.

"And I'll search the rest of the lake." Sabrina tried to look cheerful as she wove her way through her guests.

The Sapphire Princess gestured for the orchestra to play. One by one the masked guests began dancing again.

"Should I have Titus bring you a leaf boat?" Zazz asked.

Sabrina shook her head. "I'll never be able to catch her in that. I have to fly. But

I'll need my magic dust. It's in my room."

On the day she was crowned the Sapphire Princess, the great Wizard Gallivant gave Sabrina a purse full of magic dust. With it, she could fly.

When she reached her room, Sabrina stopped to look at the shell Atlanta had given her. She found her magic purse and tied it around her waist. Then she touched the beautiful pink-and-gold shell and felt a strange tingling in her fingers.

"What?"

Sabrina stared hard at the shell. When she had put it to her ear before, she had heard the ocean. When she had asked to hear the people of the Undersea, she had actually heard the voices of Atlanta's sisters. If the shell was truly magical, could it help her find Atlanta?

"I wonder," Sabrina murmured.

Sabrina lifted the shell to her ear. "Please, magic shell, where is my friend Atlanta?"

At first there was only the sound of water lapping against a shore. Then Sabrina heard the rush of falling water. It beat out a pretty melody as it fell upon the rocks. Sabrina's eyes widened. "That's Bluebonnet Falls!"

The noise of the waterfall grew louder.

"Is Atlanta there?" she asked the shell.

She was answered by the sound of someone crying.

"That sounds like Atlanta!" Sabrina lowered the shell. "I must fly to her right away."

Still holding the shell, Sabrina went to her window.

"Not so fast!" a voice growled from behind her.

She turned and gasped.

A very strange little creature with big pointy ears and bushy green eyebrows stood in her door. His green hair hung like stringy seaweed around his face. He had webbed fingers with long yellow fingernails. And he wore a gold jacket just like the one she'd seen at the costume party. Could he be Atlanta's creature after all?

"Give me shell!" he ordered.

"Who and what are you?" Sabrina asked, clutching the shell to her chest.

"Me a Sea Troll," he replied. "And that my shell."

Sabrina blinked in surprise. "You must be mistaken. This shell is mine. It was given to me as a gift."

"No gift," the Sea Troll said, shaking his head. "That shell mine. Give it back now."

Sabrina shook her head. "No."

"What!" The Sea Troll stamped his feet. "Me mad. Me take shell."

He jumped at Sabrina. His sharp fingernails scraped her hand.

"Ow!" Sabrina leaped backward onto her windowsill. She took a pinch of magic dust from her purse. As she tossed it over herself, the Sapphire Princess cried:

"Up in the air and into the sky,
Away from this Troll, let me fly!"

The Sea Troll tried to catch her, but he was too late. Sabrina was already flying high above Blue Lake.

6

The Sea Troll

The Sapphire Princess flew as fast as she could toward Bluebonnet Falls. She felt terrible.

Atlanta was telling the truth! A Sea Troll had been following the Mermaid, and Sabrina had not believed her. To make matters worse, Sabrina had embarrassed her friend in front of all of the party guests.

The Princess glanced down to make sure the Sea Troll wasn't following her, then rounded the bend to Bluebonnet Falls. As soon as she passed the Willow-That-Weeps, Sabrina heard the musical sound of the falls.

Crystal-clear water tumbled over mossy green rocks into a deep pool of blue. A rainbow painted its colors across the mist-covered water.

"A rainbow?" Sabrina murmured. "Then Atlanta must be around here someplace."

Sabrina landed in a soft green patch of grass. She was afraid to call out, for fear the Sea Troll might hear her voice and follow it. So the princess looked for Atlanta in silence.

The Mermaid wasn't in the pool at the

base of the falls. She wasn't at the top of the falls. There was only one place she could be — behind the falls.

Sabrina took a deep breath and dove through the gushing water.

When the princess came up for air, a pebble flew past her head. She was in a dark cave. And someone was throwing rocks at her!

"Stop that!" Sabrina cried, covering her head.

"Go away," a voice shouted from the darkness. "Next time I won't miss."

"Atlanta?" the princess called. "It's me, Sabrina."

Atlanta swam out of the shadows. She held a rock in one hand and a bamboo stick in the other. "Go away," Atlanta hissed. "This is my hiding place."

"Atlanta, I want to apologize."

"You should," Atlanta replied. "Why didn't you keep my secret?"

"I didn't believe there was a little creature following you."

Atlanta lowered her stick. "You didn't believe me?"

Sabrina swam closer. "But now I do. I saw the creature up close. He's a Sea Troll."

"A Sea Troll!" Atlanta repeated. "But that's impossible. Sea Trolls live in the Undersea. They're our friends."

"This Troll didn't look friendly," Sabrina said. "In fact he looked very scary."

Atlanta nodded. "Trolls used to be the enemies of our people. They lived in the lava caves and under coral bridges and attacked anyone who dared to come near them. But that was a long time ago."

"Were they captured?" Sabrina asked, wide-eyed.

"No," Atlanta replied. "King Oceanus made friends with them. Now they help him rule his kingdom."

"What do they do?" Sabrina asked.

"Trolls make very good guards," Atlanta replied. "They hide and watch. They're extremely good at hiding."

"They must be," Sabrina said. "I've never ever seen one until today. But what do they watch for?"

"Thieves," a voice growled from above them. "Thieves who steal shells."

Both girls looked up. There, tucked into one of the cracks in the ceiling of the cave, was a tiny man with big pointy ears, sharp teeth, and shiny yellow eyes.

"Me want my shell!"

Keep Away, Kelp!

 The Sapphire Princess grabbed the bamboo stick from Atlanta's hands. "You stay away from us," she shouted at the Sea Troll. "If you come any closer, I'll hit you with this stick."

The Sea Troll scampered down the rocks of the cave but kept a safe distance away. "Me want my shell."

"It isn't yours." Sabrina kept the stick in

front of her as she looked at Atlanta. "Tell him you gave me the shell."

Atlanta swam close to Sabrina. "That shell was a gift from the Undersea," she told the Sea Troll.

"No, no, no!" The Sea Troll shook his head. "That shell mine."

"It couldn't be," Atlanta shouted. "That shell came from the Undersea Palace."

"What?" Sabrina looked confused. "You told me you found it."

"I did," Atlanta said quickly. "I just didn't find it at the bottom of the ocean. I found it in the Room of Treasures."

Sabrina held up the shell. "Then this shell was stolen?"

Atlanta pursed her lips. "Well . . ."

"That right," the Sea Troll growled. He

hopped to the edge of the water. "Now give me shell."

Sabrina started to hand the Sea Troll the shell, but Atlanta dove in front of her.

"What are you doing?" Atlanta cried. "You don't even know this creature."

The Sea Troll put his hands on his hips and puffed out his chest. "Me guard at palace!"

"That's a lie," Atlanta shouted at the little man.

The Sea Troll curled his lip at her. "Me tell truth. You one who lies."

"Oh!" Atlanta's mouth dropped open. "How could you say such a thing!"

The Sea Troll shrugged. "Everyone say it."

Atlanta folded her arms across her

chest and faced Sabrina. "Who are you going to believe?"

Sabrina was torn. She knew she should believe her friend. But there was a lot of truth in what the little Sea Troll said.

"Oh, Atlanta." Sabrina climbed onto a rock between the other two. "I want to believe you, but you've lied so many times, I don't know what to think."

Atlanta's eyes were huge. "When did I lie?"

This was hard for Sabrina, but she knew she had to say it. "When you told Titus you saw a Two-Headed Snag and a Monstrous Grinder."

"I really thought I saw them," Atlanta explained. "But they were just a pair of eels and a bunch of coral."

"But what about the ball?" Sabrina

asked. "You said you saw this Sea Troll at the ball."

"'That true," the Sea Troll admitted. "I there."

Atlanta put her hands on her hips. "See? I told the truth."

Sabrina took a deep breath. "Then what about the magic shell? You said you were hunting for a Snapping Lurch when you found it."

Atlanta looked embarrassed. "I did fib a little about the Snapping Lurch," she confessed. "And I didn't tell the whole truth about where I found the shell. But I don't exaggerate all the time."

The Sea Troll pointed at the Mermaid. "Admit you stole shell from Room of Treasures."

Atlanta touched Sabrina's hand. "I'll

admit it. But I didn't think I was stealing it. There were so many treasures there that I thought one wouldn't be missed."

"Kelp guard shell," the Sea Troll declared. "Kelp miss shell."

"Kelp?" Atlanta repeated. "I've heard of a Sea Troll named Kelp."

"That me." The Sea Troll poked his chest with his thumb. "Kelp guard Room of Treasures."

Atlanta narrowed her eyes. "But where were you when I visited the Room of Treasures?"

The Sea Troll kicked at a rock with one of his webbed feet. "Kelp asleep. But Kelp wake up fast. And follow."

The Sapphire Princess sighed and folded her hands over the shell in her lap. At last, things were starting to be clear.

"I think we know the whole truth now," she said to the Sea Troll and the Mermaid. "Atlanta, you took the shell from the Room of Treasures because you wanted to give me a special gift."

Atlanta nodded. "That's right."

"And Kelp?" Sabrina smiled at the Sea Troll. "You followed Atlanta because you wanted to put the shell back where it belonged."

"Right," Kelp barked.

"I shouldn't have taken the shell," Atlanta said. "I'm sorry."

"Kelp sorry, too," the Troll replied. "Need to stay awake on job."

Sabrina turned to the Mermaid. "So, my friend, I want you to tell me what I should do with this shell."

"Give it to Kelp," Atlanta said firmly.

With the shell, Sabrina approached the

little Sea Troll. "Here's the shell," she said. "Guard it well."

The Sea Troll jumped in the air and clicked his heels. "Kelp happy. Kelp have shell back."

He dove through the waterfall and was gone.

"Wait!" Sabrina swam through the falls after him. "You didn't say good-bye."

"Sea Trolls are good at hiding and watching," Atlanta explained as she swam up beside Sabrina. "But they're not very good at manners."

Sabrina laughed and took her friend by the hand. "And speaking of manners, may I be the first to invite you back to the costume ball at my palace?"

The Mermaid bowed to the princess. "I'd be honored."

The Simple Gift

When the Sapphire Princess and the Mermaid returned to the palace, Zazz and Titus were waiting to greet them.

Zazz buzzed in a circle around Sabrina's head. "The party is so much fun. I've brought your masks and costumes. The guests are all anxious to talk to Atlanta."

"She's happy to talk to them," Sabrina said.

Just then, Titus stepped forward. "Atlanta from the Undersea, welcome to the Sapphire Palace," he boomed in his big Strider voice.

"Oh, Titus," Atlanta gushed. "I'm so sorry I ran away from you this morning. I asked Sabrina to tell you I wasn't here and then I hid in her bathtub. And then things got very confusing."

"Really?" Titus looked at the Sapphire Princess.

Sabrina nodded. "But everything's fine now. I wasn't honest with you this morning, Titus. But Atlanta and I both plan to tell the complete truth from now on."

The old guard scratched the tuft on the top of his head. "I'm not quite sure I understand."

"I think I can explain." The Mermaid

took a deep breath. "You see, I was being chased by a ferocious Sea Troll — "

"Atlanta!" Sabrina warned.

The Mermaid put one hand to her mouth. "Oops, I forgot. I promised not to exaggerate one little bit. Even if it does make a better story."

Sabrina draped one arm across the Mermaid's shoulder and grinned at Titus. "We'll just tell you the short, dull version of our story. Atlanta is here. I'm here. We all feel wonderful. And we're ready to enjoy the ball!"

Titus bowed. "That's a grand idea, Princess. I'll speak to the orchestra."

The guard hurried toward the palace garden and told the orchestra to play a lively tune.

Zazz flew after him. "Let the dancing begin!" she squeaked.

Once the two girls were alone, Atlanta said, "Sabrina, I want to give you a gift."

Sabrina raised one hand. "Oh, dear, no. Think of the trouble the last gift caused."

Atlanta laughed. "This gift is very simple. And I really did find it. Not while hunting for a Snapping Lurch, but while I was out for a swim."

Sabrina watched as Atlanta took a small fan-shaped shell from her hair. "I've had this seashell since I was a baby," she explained. "It's not very big, and it has no magic."

"But it's so beautiful!" Sabrina took the pale pink shell and tucked it into her own hair. "I'll keep it as a memory of our adventure."

"Our very big adventure," Atlanta added.

"When Atlanta the Mermaid and

Sabrina the Princess met Kelp the . . ."
Sabrina paused. She didn't want to exaggerate anything. But she did want to tell a good story.

Finally Atlanta said, "When they met Kelp the grumpy Sea Troll, and learned the importance of always telling — "

Sabrina chimed in loudly, "The truth!"

About the Authors

JAHNNA N. MALCOLM stands for Jahnna "and" Malcolm. Jahnna Beecham and Malcolm Hillgartner are married and write together. They have written over seventy books for kids. Jahnna N. Malcolm have written about ballerinas, horses, ghosts, singing cowgirls, and green slime.

Before Jahnna and Malcolm wrote books, they were actors. They met on the stage where Malcolm was playing a prince. And they were married on the stage where Jahnna was playing a princess.

Now they have their own little prince and princess: Dash and Skye. They all live in Ashland, Oregon, with their big red dog, Ruby, and their fluffy little white dog, Clarence.

Visit the authors' Web site at http://www.jewelkingdom.com.